P9-DKF-975

Henny Penny

Typeset in Bernhard Modern

Published by Bloomsbury Publishing, New York, London, and Berlin
Distributed to the trade by Holtzbrinck Publishers

Library of Congress Cataloging-in-Publication Data
French, Vivian.
Henny Penny/Vivian French & Sophie Windham
p. cm
Summary: Henny Penny and her barnyard friends are on their way to tell the king that the
sky is falling when they meet a hungry fox, but Henny Penny's quick thinking saves the day.
ISBN-10: 1 58234 706 9 • ISBN-13: 978 1 58234 706 6
(1. Folklore.) Windham, Sophie, ill. II. Chicken Licken. III. Title
PZ8.3.F909Hen 2006 398.2—dc2 2(E) 2005053688

First U.S. Edition 2006
Printed in China
3 5 7 9 10 8 6 4

Bloomsbury Publishing, Children's Books, U.S.A.
175 Fifth Avenue, New York, NY 10010

All papers used by Bloomsbury Publishing are natural, recyclable products made from wood grown in well-managed forests.
The manufacturing processes conform to the environmental regulations of the country of origin.

Henny Penny

Vivian French • illustrated by Sophie Windham

For Simon with much love
V.F.

For Willow
S.W.

Now, you may have already heard the story of Henny Penny, and you may have been told how her foolishness led her to a terrible end.
That, I promise you, is not the real story.
That is the story the foxes like to tell.
This is the true story, the story of what really happened after the acorn fell from the oak tree.

How do I know?
Because Henny Penny told me.

Henny Penny was busy in her kitchen making a big corn cake.

She mixed it, she whisked it, she stirred it, and she put it
in the oven to bake.

"There," said Henny Penny, "What a delicious cake that will be! But, oh dear me! There's cornmeal everywhere!" And she picked up a dustcloth and began to dust.

"ATCHOO!" sneezed Henny Penny. "ATCHOO! I must take my dustcloth outside and shake it."

She hurried outside to shake her dustcloth this way and that, round and round, and as she was shaking it . . .

PLOP!

An acorn fell from the oak tree and landed on Henny Penny's head.

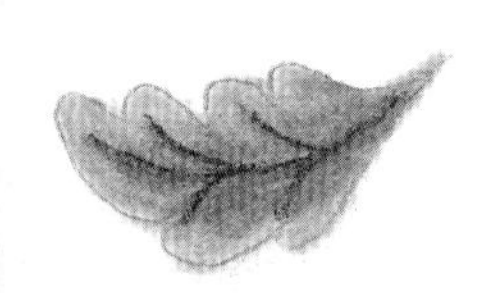

"Cluck, cluck, CLUCK!" clucked Henny Penny.
"Mercy, mercy me! I do believe the sky is falling!

Whatever shall I do? I must go and tell the king!"
And Henny Penny stuffed her dustcloth into her pocket and
set off down the road.

She hadn't gone far when she met Ducky Lucky.
"Hello, Henny Penny," said Ducky Lucky.
"You seem to be in a terrible hurry. Where are you going?"

"Oh, Ducky Lucky!" said Henny Penny. "I was shaking my dustcloth this way and that, round and round, and all of a sudden the sky fell down! And I don't know what to do, so I'm going to tell the king."

"Quack, quack, QUACK!" quacked Ducky Lucky. "If the sky is falling, I'd better come with you."

So Henny Penny and Ducky Lucky pit-pit-pattered down the road together.

They hadn't gone very far when they met Cocky Locky.

"Hello, Henny Penny," said Cocky Locky. "Hello, Ducky Lucky. You seem to be in a terrible hurry. Where are you going?"

"Oh, Cocky Locky!" said Henny Penny. "I was shaking my dustcloth this way and that, round and round, and all of a sudden the sky fell down! I don't know what to do, so we're going to tell the king."

"Cock-a-doodle-DOO!" crowed Cocky Locky. "If the sky is falling, I'd better come with you."

So Henny Penny, Ducky Lucky, and Cocky Locky pit-pit-pattered down the road together.

They hadn't gone far when they met Goosey Loosey.
"Hello, Henny Penny," said Goosey Loosey. "Hello, Ducky Lucky and Cocky Locky.
You seem to be in a terrible hurry. Where are you going?"

"Oh, Goosey Loosey!" said Henny Penny. "I was shaking my dustcloth this way and that, round and round, and all of a sudden the sky fell down!
I don't know what to do, so we're going to tell the king."

"Hiss, hiss, HISS!" hissed Goosey Loosey. "If the sky is falling, I'd better come with you."
So Henny Penny, Ducky Lucky, Cocky Locky, and Goosey Loosey pit-pit-pattered down the road together.

They hadn't gone far when they met Turkey Lurkey.
"Hello, Henny Penny," said Turkey Lurkey. "Hello, Ducky Lucky, Cocky Locky, and Goosey Loosey. You seem to be in a terrible hurry. Where are you going?"

"Oh, Turkey Lurkey!" said Henny Penny. "I was shaking my dustcloth this way and that, round and round, and all of a sudden the sky fell down! I don't know what to do, so we're going to tell the king."

"Gobble, gobble, GOBBLE!" gobbled Turkey Lurkey. "If the sky is falling, I'd better come with you."

So Henny Penny, Ducky Lucky, Cocky Locky, Goosey Loosey, and Turkey Lurkey pit-pit-pattered down the road together.

They hadn't gone far when they met Foxy Loxy.

"Well, well, well," said Foxy Loxy. "Who have we here? Henny Penny, Ducky Lucky, Cocky Locky, Goosey Loosey, and Turkey Lurkey, if my old eyes don't deceive me. And where are you going in such a hurry?"

"Oh, Foxy Loxy!" said Henny Penny. "I was shaking my dustcloth this way and that, round and round, and all of a sudden the sky fell down! We don't know what to do, so we're going to tell the king."

“How sensible you are, Henny Penny,” said Foxy Loxy, and he smiled a sharp-toothed smile. “And do you know which way to go?”

Henny Penny stopped and thought about it.

“How silly I am,” she said. “No, I don’t!”

“Then let me show you,” said Foxy Loxy. “Just follow me.”

So Henny Penny, Ducky Lucky, Cocky Locky, Goosey Loosey, and Turkey Lurkey pit-pit-pattered after Foxy Loxy.

Foxy Loxy led them through the grass . . .

under the trees . . .

and in and out of the bushes . . .

until suddenly —

they were in a dusty-musty kitchen in a dusty-musty house. Foxy Loxy shut the door behind them.

"Gobble, gobble, gobble!" said Turkey Lurkey.
"Is this where the king lives?"
"No, my dears," said Foxy Loxy. "This is *my* house. I thought
we could all have a lovely dinner before we see the king.
Just sit yourselves down, and I'll light the fire."

Ducky Lucky settled in front of the hearth.
Cocky Locky perched on a chair.
Goosey Loosey and Turkey Lurkey flapped up to the sofa.

Henny Penny stood very
still and looked around.

She saw feathers
on the floor.

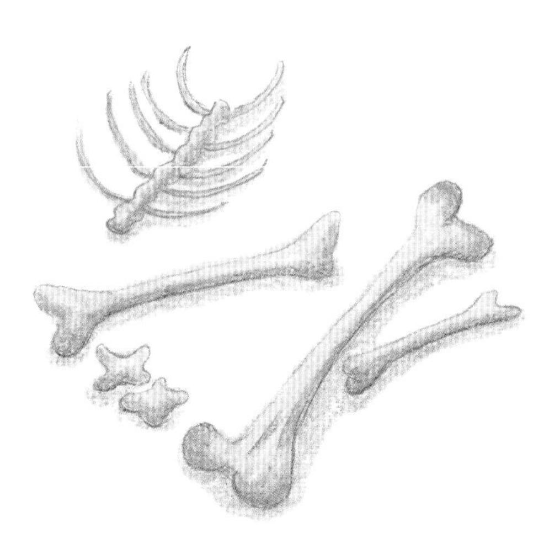

She saw a pile of old
bones in the corner.

She saw Foxy Loxy putting
a BIG pot of water
on the roaring fire.

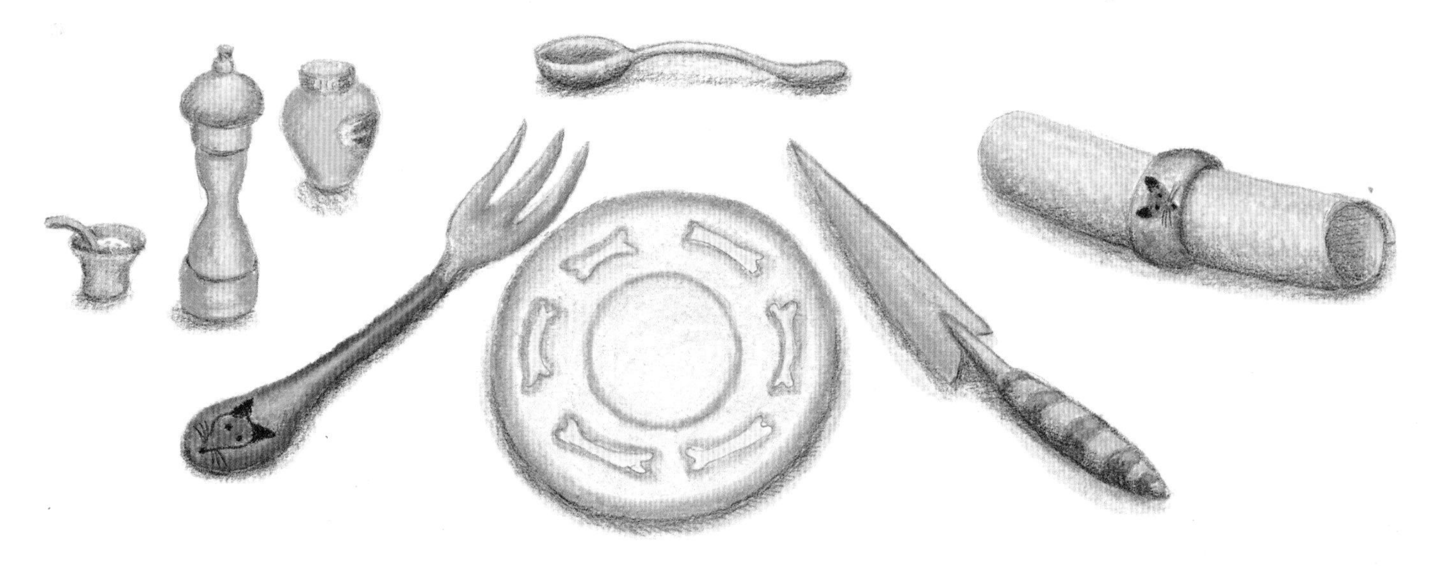

And she saw him set the table with one fork, one plate, and one big, sharp knife.

Henny Penny felt nervous . . . but she shook her head and fluffed up her feathers. "Now, Henny Penny," she said to herself. "You may be silly, but surely there's something you can do."

And Henny Penny
had an idea.

"Oh, Foxy Loxy!" said Henny Penny. "What a mess! What a muddle! *Do* let me tidy up around here!"

And she pulled her dustcloth out of her pocket.

Foxy Loxy was VERY surprised. "Eh . . . what?" he said.

Ducky Lucky, Cocky Locky, Goosey Loosey, and Turkey Lurkey stared at Henny Penny.

"*Gobble, gobble, gobble!* What about our dinner?" said Turkey Lurkey.

“Let’s make Foxy Loxy comfortable first,” Henny Penny said. “Now, Foxy Loxy, you sit down and take a little rest. I’ll give your room a polish. We’ll wake you up when it’s clean and tidy.”

Foxy Loxy stroked his whiskers. His house certainly was messy, now that he looked around.

"Very well then," he said. "But be sure to wake me the moment you've finished!"

"*Gobble, gobble, gobble!*" said Turkey Lurkey. "Then we'll all have dinner!"

"We certainly will," said Foxy Loxy. He licked his lips and curled up in his comfiest chair.

Henny Penny began to dust. As she dusted she began to sing:

"Hush, Mr. Foxy, and close your eyes,
soon you'll be having a special surprise."

"*Gobble, gobble, gobble!*" said Turkey Lurkey. "Will we have a surprise, too?"

Foxy Loxy opened one eye. "Oh, yes," he said, and his belly rumbled. "You'll have a BIG surprise, Turkey Lurkey!"

"Shh, Turkey Lurkey!" said Henny Penny, and she went on dusting and singing.

"Hush, Mr. Foxy, and close your eyes, soon you'll be having a special surprise"

Foxy Loxy sighed and closed his eyes. Henny Penny went on dusting and singing.

Foxy Loxy began to snore.

Henny Penny quietly, quietly, quietly,
opened the door and Ducky Lucky, Cocky
Locky, and Goosey Loosey tiptoed out.
"Gobble, gobble, gobble!" said Turkey Lurkey.
"What about my surprise?"

Foxy Loxy grunted in his sleep.
"Turkey Lurkey," whispered Henny Penny,
"if you don't tiptoe out, Foxy Loxy
will give you a great big TERRIBLE
surprise — he'll eat *you* for dinner!"

"GOBBLE, GOBBLE, GOBBLE!" shouted Turkey Lurkey. He flapped, flurried, and flounced through the door just as fast as he could, and Henny Penny flew after him.

Foxy Loxy woke up just as the door banged shut behind them!

Turkey Lurkey, Goosey Loosey, Cocky Locky, and
Ducky Lucky ran all the way to Henny Penny's house.
There was a wonderful smell of corn cake as Henny Penny
opened the door to let them in.

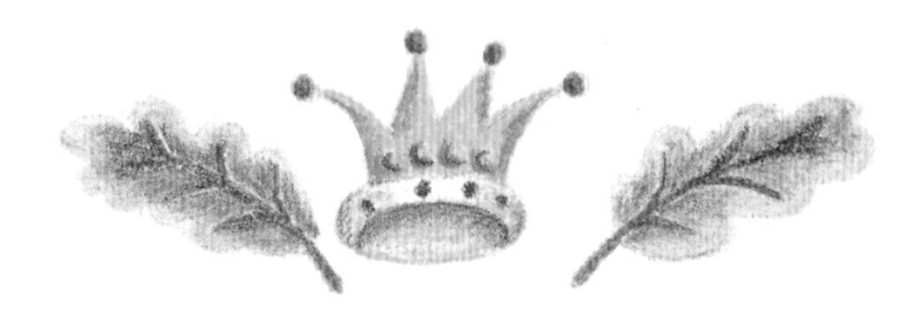

"I don't think we'll bother the king today," Henny Penny said.
"Let's have a slice of corn cake instead."

And that, as Turkey Lurkey said, was the best surprise of all.